BEYOND THE WOODLAND

JERSEY, CHANNEL ISLANDS

BY
ALEXANDRA KETTLES

CW00828771

Writer	Alexandra Kettles
Illustrator	Stephen Hoffe
Editor	Milena Wolmarans

ACKNOWLEDGEMENTS

Special thanks to Robert and Milena for their continued support and encouragement.

This book is dedicated to my dearest mother whom I owe much gratitude for her kindness, patience, support, and unconditional love throughout my life.

Thank you for your guidance and when we don't see eye to eye, the laughter, hugs and dances.

Contents

1

The Arrival, St Peters Jersey

"Can you see Eva yet, Tom?" I called to my brother as I helped dad pull a suitcase off the conveyor belt.

"I can't see anything through that door, Charlotte," Tom replied excitedly, racing back to join them. He gently picked up Charlotte's rucksack and placed it on to his back.

My mobile beeped but I didn't check it. Tom and I were too busy weaving through the crowd trying to see past the automatic doors.

"There she is, over there," Tom pointed.

"Oooo, I just can't wait!" I squealed,

grabbing hold of his arm.

"Me too!" Tom's smile turned to a worried frown as he whispered into my ear, "These Goobies are wriggling about too much! I hope no one notices." He gazed around suspiciously.

"Walk confidently, Tom. We're nearly there."

We marched through the automatic doors and headed straight toward Eva and her family. She had the broadest smile. Tom and I were grinning too.

I tried to catch Eva's attention in the bustle of greetings. Tom was a great distraction without even knowing it as he excitedly told everyone of his adventurous flight.

"I fell in the aisle and, and, and..." his words rushed out.

I was no longer listening. There were too many voices and no matter how much I gestured to Eva, I couldn't get my message across without everyone hearing.

She was looking quite baffled.

Eva sidled up to me. "What are you trying to say?"

"I'll tell you in the car," I smiled, giving her a big hug. "It's so lovely to see you! Can you travel with us? Dad's hired a car."

"I'd love to."

Eva's parents paid for the parking and we were all walking out of the airport when Tom stopped. His eyes sparkled, his mouth opened, and both his feet left the ground as he leapt into the air.

"Whooooa!" he burst out. "What is that?" he asked wide-eyed, pointing with both hands.

Near the exit stood a huge painted statue. It was almost double the height of Tom!

"Oh," Eva giggled. "It's part of an orangutan hunt across the island to raise funds for the zoo. It's a big competition. There's fifty-two to find."

"That sounds like fun!" Tom said, taking a photo with his wristwatch.

"Let's do the hunt," I grinned.

"Yes, let's," agreed Eva, beaming.

A mobile beeped again.

"Check it, Charlotte!" Tom said, seriously. "It could be important."

"It's from Dan. He's just asking if we are okay."

I stopped to send a quick message back.

LANDED. ALL OK. WILL B IN
TOUCH LATER. LOTS TO TELL.
C, T & E

"Come on, Charlotte!" dad urged, "Put your rucksack in the boot!"

"No, it's okay dad. I'll keep it with me," I answered him, hoping he wouldn't mind.

He looked concerned.

"Really? It might be a little squashed in the back."

"Yes, really, I'm okay with it. Thanks dad."

I ducked quickly into the back seat, poking Tom so he would shift up. We held our breath afraid dad would object, but he clunked the boot shut and we sighed in relief. Eva looked at us quizzically. I knew it wasn't safe to talk yet so I shook my head.

Dad climbed into the driver's seat and turned the radio on. As music filled our ears, I leaned over Tom and whispered to Eva.

"The Goobies are here!"

Her eyes widened in surprise. "What?"

"We found them in my rucksack on the plane. They escaped and poor Tom got caught trying to save them. That's why he tripped and landed in the aisle."

Eva gasped, "Oh, nooo! Is that what you were talking about earlier, Tom?"

Tom nodded energetically.

Eva's hands flew to her face, "Did anybody see them?"

"I think I got there in time," Tom beamed. "They're in Charlotte's rucksack now."

"We discovered they eat pony cubes!" I said, taking a few from the side pocket of my bag.

"D'you have any at home, Eva?" Tom asked. "We will have to buy some if not."

Eva shrugged, "I have no idea. We might have to go to the pet shop." Her eyes widened, "No, no, no! My aunt has a stable yard. I'm sure she'll have cubes."

We all grinned at each other. We had no idea what else to feed them.

I could feel them moving in the rucksack on my lap. They were restless. I didn't know what to do, so I cradled the bag gently and hoped they would settle.

"Look!" Tom said as he bounced in his seat, looking taller than usual. "Look! It's the sea."

As dad drove up the steep hill and turned the hairpin bend, a spectacular view came into sight. Tom strained against his seatbelt to get a better look. Bright, blue waters stretched out before us as far as our eyes could see. Jagged rocks jutted across the shoreline offering a stark contrast to the sandy beaches around them.

"It's low tide," mum commented from the front. She glanced back and smiled at us, "We will plan a beach trip as soon as we have settled in."

It took ten minutes to reach Eva's house.

"It's big," Tom marvelled as we pulled into the driveway.

"I'm so glad we are here!" I whispered, "The Goobies are desperate to get out!"

"Come on, Charlotte," said Eva, taking my hand. "You too, Tom! I'll show you around." As we began to race up the wooden steps, we heard someone calling…

"Hello, hello, hello!"

A boy Tom's age came running through the front door. His right arm stretched out to support him as he came flying into the entrance hall.

"Hello," said Tom, openly admiring the newcomers' style of arrival.

"Oh, hi Charlie! This is Charlotte and Tom." Eva introduced us. "They have come to stay for a few days."

"Hello Charlie," Paige called from the lounge.

"Hello, Mrs Parsons." He turned to Charlotte and Tom, grinning, "Nice to meet you both."

Tom and Charlie began to chat when I felt my rucksack move.

"Eva, we really need to get to your room!" I urged her under my breath.

"Sorry! Yes, of course!" she hesitated, "Uum… what about Charlie?"

I looked at her pleadingly and hoped she understood. I didn't really know who Charlie was, let alone whether he could be trusted to keep the Goobies a secret.

Eva's quick thinking came to our rescue.

"Charlie, can you take Tom to see the pool?"

"But but…" protested Tom.

"No buts, Tom. It's for the best!" I interrupted.

I ran up the steps after Eva, who was already nearing the top.

"I hope the boys aren't angry at us." Eva looked worried. "Did we do the right thing?"

"I don't think we were mean. Wait… do you think we should tell Charlie?"

"It is quite a big secret, Charlotte." She bit her bottom lip, "I think we can trust Charlie."

We decided right there and then to tell him about the Goobies. Racing to the top of the stairs, we shouted…

CHARLIEEE! TOOOOM!

… but it was too late. They were nowhere to be seen.

Knowing the Goobies were still in my bag, we both hastened to Eva's room to check on them.

2

A Goobie in my Hand

I fully intended to open my rucksack and let the Goobies out, but as we entered Eva's room, I found myself staring. Her room was so beautiful! The turquoise duvet matched the window blind, which was patterned with robins and delicate, white flowers. A large painting of blue butterflies in flight hung on her wall next to a world map that Eva had marked with all the places she had visited.

"Come on!" Eva jolted me back to the present as she closed the door.

"I'll shut the window. I love your room, Eva."

I walked to the window and spotted Tom and Charlie in the garden below.

"Tom! Charlie!" I shouted, cheerfully.

I pushed the window open and began to wave, when, to my horror, my rucksack slipped off my right shoulder and fell through the window!

"Watch out!" Eva ran towards me, reaching for the bag… it slipped through her fingers.

"Thoooooomas!!!!!" I shouted.

Tom looked up and saw the rucksack falling, but he was too far to catch it.

"Charlie, catch the bag!"

"I can't look," Eva said, covering her eyes.

"Me neither, Eva…… aaargh!"

Quickly crossing my fingers and squeezing my eyes tightly shut, we held our breaths, waiting for the thud from below.

'I've got it!" Charlie chirped.

I opened my eyes to see him holding up the rucksack, beaming with pride.

"Ooo," I shrieked, "Thank you, Charlie!"

Eva sighed with relief.

Tom zoomed past Charlie shouting, "Let's get upstairs, quick!"

Eva and I raced to the door and swung it open. The boys were fast! They were almost at the top of the stairs.

Charlie looked confused, "What's the hurry?"

"Come on!" Eva ushered him into her room.

"Can you keep a secret?" I asked.

"Of course! What's going on?"

I caught a glimpse of Tom from the corner of my eye. He looked worried.

"I hope they aren't hurt," he whispered.

Charlie frowned, "What are you talking about?"

I gently took the bag from Charlie and nodded to Tom. His frown suddenly turned into a big smile and he launched into the story of how we discovered the

Goobies. Charlie was enthralled. Especially when Tom told him that the Goobies were hidden in the rucksack he had caught!

"Are they okay? Can I see? How small are they? Will they run away?" a barrage of questions came tumbling out.

"Open the bag, Charlotte!" prompted Tom.

"Okaaaay! Are you ready?"

"Yes, yes! Do it," encouraged Eva.

I sat quietly on the bed with my bag in my lap and unzipped it.

I opened it a little...

... nothing happened.

I opened it wider...

... still nothing.

"W-where are they?" Tom quietly asked. "You don't think they're... dead, do you, Charlotte?" Tom's eyes glistened.

We all sat down, staring at the bag.

The room was silent. I was too scared to look inside.

Eva nudged me, "Go on, Charlotte."

I placed the open rucksack next to me on the bed and peered in. The Goobies were a ball of feathers at the bottom. A lifeless ball of feathers and fur. I slowly put my hand inside and gently picked one up.

"Look!" I said, stretching out my arm…

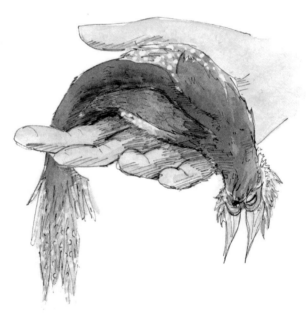

… the Goobie lay motionless…

Charlie was spellbound.

"Is it alive, Charlotte?" Eva asked.

"I'm not sure. Come closer, Eva. Help me."

"I'll help, but I don't really know what to do."

I peered at the Goobie lying draped across my hand. "Look how beautiful it is," I marvelled. "Purple, almost black fur and yellow on the tips of its feathers. There's even white spots!"

"I think it's breathing! I saw its body move. Yes," Eva said, confidently, "it is breathing. Quickly, take the other Goobie out."

"I'll get it!" Tom, jumping up, reached for the rucksack.

"Gently," I cautioned him.

He quickly pulled his arm back, wriggled his whole body about, took a deep breath and tried again. As Tom's hand emerged from the rucksack, a small, open-eyed Goobie stared up at him.

A faint sound filled the room…

I held the Goobie close to my chest, hoping my heartbeat would be comforting.

Tom, with both hands, lightly placed his Goobie on Eva's bed.

My mobile beeped.

I set the Goobie down next to its friend, "There you go little one." I turned to Eva, "Do you have a blanket and perhaps a small bowl for water?"

"Yes, I can use one of the cat bowls," she said, hurrying out the room.

We sat on the floor next to the bed watching the Goobies until Eva returned.

"I brought two bowls. One for water and one for food. Come on! Let's set up a cosy place for them in my wardrobe."

"Brilliant. I'll get the last of the food," Tom offered, rummaging around in my bag.

We all grinned at each other as we settled the Goobies into their new home.

They had made the journey.

"Charlie!" someone called from the hall.

Charlie's hands flew to his mouth. "That's my mum! I don't want to go! I just don't want to."

"Go on, Charlie. You better hurry. We'll see you tomorrow morning."

"Maybe you can keep me company?" Tom suggested, "I'm always the first up."

"Deal!" Charlie shook Tom's hand. "Bye," he waved as he headed towards the stairs.

We watched from the bedroom door as he reluctantly descended one step at a time. We waved a final good-bye before disappearing back into the bedroom and closing the door.

The Goobies had fallen asleep all curled up.

What an enchanted magical moment.

3

Aunt Zara Comes for Dinner

"Eva!" Paige called. "Aunty Zara is coming for dinner tonight. Can you help to lay the table for ten, please?"

Eva rolled her eyes and her shoulders sank as she answered, "Coming mum." She dragged her feet reluctantly taking each step in subtle defiance of having to do a chore.

We both followed her to the dining room, making sure to close the bedroom door behind us.

To my surprise, the dining room table was set in a large glass conservatory that led off the lounge. A light wooden shelf, that almost ran the length of the room, housed a variety of the tallest orchids I'd ever seen.

We began to lay the table.

Tom slouched, "I'm bored."

"Go see what dad's doing."

He tilted his head to the side and looked up towards the ceiling in thought. Spinning around on the spot he said, "see you later," and raced out the room.

As Tom was leaving, two cats confidently sauntered in. One was ginger and the other had unusual markings.

"What type of cat is that?"

"Oh, Naliyah? She is a Bengal cat."

"I haven't seen a cat like her before. How do you say her name again?"

"Na-li-yah," Eva enunciated, "and the ginger one is Tippen." She pointed, "See the white tip on her tail?"

"Oh yes," I smiled. "May I stroke them?"

"Go ahead! They love the attention but don't pick them up," she cautioned.

My mobile beeped.

"Gosh, poor Danny. I forgot to update him."

"You better reply, Charlotte."

The doorbell rang.

"Come on! Come and meet Aunt Zara. She's great fun!"

I sent Dan a quick text.

> ARRIVED @ EVA'S. GOOBIES
> HAD A FALL. MADE A BED 4
> THEM IN EVA'S WARDROBE.
> CHAT SOON. C,T & E

I put my mobile on the table and ran to the front door with Eva. Tom came skidding around the corner and almost bumped into Katie in the corridor. I shoved him playfully.

"Hello Aunt Zara. How are you?" Eva beamed, giving her aunt a giant hug. "These are my friends, Charlotte and Tom."

"Hello poppet," she replied, pinching Katie's cheek. Aunt Zara shook off her coat and removed a very colourful hat, saying "My goodness, what lovely friends you have."

We grinned. Aunt Zara certainly wasn't average! She had googly eyes that her glasses couldn't quite cover, mousey brown hair streaked with grey, which was only partly tied back, and the brightest clothes I had ever seen.

"This is my friend Hanlie, from South Africa." Aunt Zara hung her coat up on the peg.

"Hiya," said Hanlie in a high-pitched, bubbly voice.

We all welcomed Hanlie warmly. The entrance was quite crowded but as the door began to close, we spotted Charlie and his parents walking up the path.

Tom beamed from ear to ear, "Charlie! Wait here, I'll be right back," he said, racing upstairs.

We had arranged shifts to keep watch over the Goobies and it was Tom's turn.

"Evening everyone, glad you could make it," Paige smiled as she met us at the door. Continuing the introductions, we all moved through to the dining room, chatting as we settled ourselves around the table. Dinner and drinks were set out, and my stomach grumbled at the sight of it all.

I was sitting opposite Aunt Zara, between Eva and her mum. Tom was, obviously, sitting next to Charlie. He had given us the all-okay signal as soon as he sat down.

Knives and forks clinked, and dishes passed across the table. The room filled with laughter.

"Could you please pass me the um, the um… what's-a-me-call-it, the thing-a-me-jig, the skoodle," Aunt Zara asked, pointing across the table.

"What is she on about?" I whispered.

"I think she wants the butter."

"Oh!" I giggled, "Why doesn't she just say that?"

"She forgets the names of things."

Aunt Zara raised her head and peered over her glasses, "I can hear you, y'know."

Everyone laughed.

"Aunt dotty if you ask me!" said Josh, winking at his aunt and rubbing at his beard.

"I haven't got a beard," Aunt Zara retorted, lifting her chin as proof.

"Is that why they call you Uncle Zara?" Eva asked. "I don't think you have a beard, but you are rather fat."

"Eva!" reprimanded Paige.

"To be fair, Eva," interrupted Tom, "she's not fat but rather plump!"

"Thomas!" … but before mum could really tell him off, the whole table roared with laughter. Even Aunt Zara!

"Talking of being plump, I'm starving! Tom, could you liven up and pass the skoodles?"

Tom's jaw dropped. No one had ever asked him to liven up before.

"Um, the potatoes?" he tilted his head.

"No," Aunt Zara's hand swayed through the air, in no particular direction, "the skoodles."

Tom tried again, "Spinach?"

"Noo, the skoodles, please!" she repeated.

I lost myself for a moment, turning the word 'skoodle' around in my head. I don't know why but I really enjoy saying it, whatever it means. I tried to pay attention while everyone around the table was still trying to work out what it was that Aunt Zara wanted.

"Ek *dink* dat sy die wortels wil hê," Hanlie said in a strange language.

Charlie frowned. "What does that mean?" he asked, curiously.

"It means, *I think she wants the carrots*," replied Aunt Zara. She sat up straighter and grinned, "Yes! Please pass the carrots!"

Everyone laughed as Tom picked up the bowl of carrots and passed them across to Aunt Zara.

31

"Skoodle and Dink… Skoodle and Dink," I quietly repeated the words to myself again and again. I glanced at Eva, "Hm… **Skoodle** and **Dink**."

"What are you talking about, Charlotte?" she laughed, looking a little puzzled.

"They're great names for the Goobies! What do you think?"

"Oooo! I love them," she whispered excitedly, nodding her head in agreement. "Skoodle and Dink!"

And just like that, the Goobies were named.

4

A Sleepless Night

"I am so exhausted - what a day! Your Aunt is so much fun!" I flopped onto the bed.

Tippen and Naliyah waltzed into the room. They arched their backs, stretching and digging their claws into the carpet.

I had forgotten to close the door.

"Charlotte!"

"Sorryyy! I completely forgot. Where are the Goobies?"

We glanced around and spotted them gliding through the air, looking left and right as they headed straight towards Tippen and Naliyah! They didn't seem afraid, but we could never really tell with the Goobies.

"We may have a fight on our hands."

I jumped up from the bed, "How can I help?"

"Try to stop the Goobies from reaching the door while I shoo the cats out!"

"On it!"

"Okay, Naliyah, off you go! You too, Tippen," Eva was ushering them out of the bedroom just as Tom was entering through the door.

"Quick, Tom, move!"

Tom looked surprised at the commotion. "What's going on?"

Despite Eva's best efforts at guiding them, the cats were caught up between Tom's legs.

"Move, Tom! Move out the way."

"Crikey! Sorry, Eva."

Lifting one leg up high to step over the cats, then repeating it with the other, Tom half-danced into the room.

"Watch out!"

Tom ducked out the way as a Goobie flew by.

Eva shut the door and collapsing to the floor with a big sigh, asked, "Where are the Goobies?"

I pointed, "One's over there and the other's next to Tom."

Tom watched the Goobie closest to him. "Which one is Skoodle and which one is Dink?"

"Let's name them. Look for a distinguishing mark, Tom."

"A what?"

"Something that one Goobie has but the other doesn't," said Eva, sitting up and taking off her socks.

"That's difficult to see from far away. Can we catch them?"

"We've tried that before haven't we, Tom?"

"I guess."

"You can't expect to befriend a wild creature or animal if you try to trap them. We learnt that last summer, remember?"

He nodded. We quietly sat on the bed together and watched the Goobies, looking for differences between them.

"Look! Look at that one's feathers. Can you see?" Eva asked, excitedly. "One feather has a green tip, and the others are yellow."

"You're right, Eva! How could we miss that?" Tom nudged his sister.

"Can this be **Skoodle**?"

"Up to you, Eva! You found the difference."

"Then the other one is **Dink**," I said, grinning.

All three of us repeated their names together, smiling at each other triumphantly.

I shifted closer to the Goobie with a green-tipped feather and started to gently call it, "Skoodle… Skoodle… Skoodle."

"Good idea!" said Eva, sitting on the floor so she could work with Dink.

"What can I do?"

"Takeover here, Tom. I must tell Danny."

WE'VE NAMED THE GOOBIES SKOODLE AND DINK. FUNNY STORY. TRYING TO TRAIN THEM NOW. C,T & E

That night, Eva and I stayed up long after Tom had gone to bed, trying to teach Skoodle and Dink their names. We didn't get undressed; we didn't go to bed. We were so tired that neither of us really remembers how the night ended.

In the morning when we woke up, Skoodle was next to my head on the pillow and Dink was tucked right up against Eva's tummy.

Both were fast asleep.

5

A Trip to Town

A knock sounded on the door.

"Eva? Charlotte? You awake?" Tom called softly from the other side.

"Just," Eva replied. "Dink is sleeping."

"Can I come in?"

"Yep," I called out. "What a night!" I yawned, stretching out my arms and legs.

Tom poked his head around the door. "We are off to town."

"Wait for us, Tom."

The sun was streaming in through a gap in the curtains. The house sounded quite noisy. Skoodle and Dink began to move. We got up carefully and hurried to dress.

Before we knew it, we were running for the car. None of us noticed Skoodle and Dink hiding behind our hair.

"I'm travelling with you guys," said Tom, running from one car to the other.

"Get in, get in!"

Tom wedged himself in between us.

I took my hair band off my wrist and gathered my hair to tie it back, when I felt something… "Huh?! … Skoodle?!"

"Eva, check your hair…" I began to say, but she was already reaching back...

Her eyes widened in surprise, "Dink!"

"Brilliant," chuckled Tom, "town is going to be fun!"

"I'm leaving my hair down."

"We don't have an option now, Eva."

"Look!" Tom pointed, spotting an orangutan.

Dad tried to stop but, no matter how hard we pleaded, he couldn't find a place to park.

"Charlotte," Eva whispered, "what do you think Skoodle and Dink will do when we leave the car?"

"We're about to find out," I answered, opening the door as dad parked the car.

Tom watch quietly.

"Eva! Tom! Charlotte!"

"Look! It's Charlie," Tom waved eagerly.

He ran ahead to say hi. We could see him whispering excitedly to Charlie as they walked back towards us. Tom tapped his arm twice and Charlie winked as we all fell in line behind our parents.

We spent too much time looking at gems, goblins and fairies, in what I called the spooky store; spent too little time visiting the toy shop; and, disappointingly, spent no time at all in the market. Skoodle and Dink had been silent the whole time. We had just turned on to Halkett Street and I was beginning to wonder if the Goobies were frightened when I heard our mum's voices rise in excitement.

I looked up to see them bee-lining towards a quaint boutique.

Pushing the creaky door open, a small bell rang... *Ting-a-ling* ...

The boutique cocooned us in quiet calm, shutting the noisy world out as soon as the door had closed. It was beautiful inside. The walls were lined with multicoloured dresses. A grey, two-seater couch beckoned to us - Eva and I hogged it.

Skoodle appeared from behind my straggly hair and in the quietest murmur *burbled* to Dink. Dink floated from Eva's shoulder and landed on the couch.

Tom and Charlie, who stood at the door reading the instructions on the packaging of their new toys, looked up to watch him. They waited... we all waited... for what, we weren't sure.

Then it happened...

"Skoodle, come back!" I called, leaping from the couch.

"Oh no! Dink, stop!"

"Charlie, they need help," Tom, clumsily dropping his toy, playfully hit Charlie in the stomach as he ran to help.

The Goobies were too fast. Before we could react, Skoodle and Dink had gracefully floated halfway across the room and landed on the floor. They slid towards the window display.

"You don't think they'll go for the red silk dress in the window, do you?" asked Eva, horrified. "Dooo something!"

"What, Eva? What can we do?" I bit my bottom lip, "We can't catch them. They'll disappear."

"Is everything alright down there?" the saleslady called down to us from the mezzanine. I could see her feet on the stairs.

We ducked into a row of clothes nearest to the display.

"We're fine! No problem," Eva called back up, raising an eye-brow at me.

"Tom and Charlie have new toys..." but before she could finish her sentence, the sales lady disappeared to help mum and Paige.

Then...

... it echoed through the shop.

The manakin fell with a thud, its head rolling away across the carpeted floor. The folds of the dress billowed out, floating slowly down.

Everyone came running.

"What happened?" mum asked.

"Is everyone okay?" added Mrs Parsons.

Eva and I scrambled to make things seem a bit more orderly than they looked, but it was too late.

"Oh! My dress," squealed the saleslady.

Charlie looked at Tom; Tom looked at Charlie.

"Think, think, think," Charlie muttered under his breath.

Everything was higgledy-piggledy.

Skoodle and Dink were nowhere to be seen.

The boys sprang into action. Charlie picked up the head, but as Tom tried to lift the body, the manakin's arm fell off.

Mum did not look impressed. She leant forward to assist the saleslady with the dress, lifting one of the delicate folds up to inspect it. To our mixed horror and relief, Skoodle and Dink dashed out from underneath and headed straight towards us. We tried to distract the adults, but everyone was so concerned with the dress that the Goobies went completely unnoticed.

Before we knew it, they were nestled safety in our hair, and we were out the door in a flash.

6

Trip to Plémont Beach

"Hit it, hit it high!"

"That's good."

"Alright, Emily! You've got this."

"Nice back up!"

"Get it, Richard!"

Shouts of teamwork filled the beach.

"Ahhhhhhh," Richard cried out, leaping forward. He overbalanced and landed in the wet sand.

"OOOoo, watch it."

"My serve! 8-14," a boy Tom's age bellowed.

"Ow, that hurt," he complained, as the returned ball bounced off of his head.

"Sorry." An older boy ruffled his hair.

"Serving…"

"Nice shot!"

"Go…"

"Ah, brilliant spike!"

"Awesome point."

They all laughed as they played.

Clap clap clap Clap clap clap Clap

"Wish we could play."

"Go ask them, Tom," I encouraged. He didn't.

The background noise washed over us as we skirted the rocks. Our feet sank into the warm dry sand. The sun shone, giving off a little heat in the gentle breeze. It was a mild day. Waves crashed lazily as they fell, fizzing into tiny white bubbles on the beach. I wrinkled my nose at the smell of seaweed then messaged Dan.

@ THE BEACH 2DAY. SKOODLE & DINK R WITH US. HOPE THEY'LL B OK WITH THE WATER. C, T & E

Skoodle and Dink were settled in our hair, burbling with content. I wondered if they were anxious.

"Let's collect sea glass," Eva suggested.

"What's sea glass?"

"It's pollution, isn't it?" Tom cut in.

"I suppose it is. It's bits of glass that are worn down by the waves and sand.

I collect them and make pictures. I can show you when we get back if you like?"

Tom nodded enthusiastically. His eyes widened in surprise as he noticed Skoodle clinging to the front of his t-shirt.

"Oh! Hi, Skoodle."

Skoodle *burbled* and floated back to my shoulder.

"They're beginning to trust us," said Eva, smiling. She picked up a dark blue piece of sea glass and put it in her bucket.

"Well, we haven't trapped them and they've been free, like all wild creatures should be."

"What about zoos?" Tom asked, sceptically.

His question prompted a discussion on the topic and we wondered the beach, chatting. No one noticed the dry, warm sand turn to moist, cold sand until the ocean's surf washed over our ankles.

"Skoodle!" I called in surprise. Dread filled the pit of my stomach as I realised how close to the ocean the Goobie was. "Skoodle!" I desperately pleaded.

Skoodle floated happily along, unaware of the waves getting larger and closer.

"Skoodle, come back!"

Dink, who now sat on Tom's arm, *burbled* and *burbled*... we could all see the danger.

Run! a voice screamed in my head. I ran so fast that my ribs hurt, barely hearing Tom and Eva behind me. Gasping in helpless horror, I watched a wave crash over Skoodle, who disappeared under the water and didn't come back up. I collapsed in the cold, wet surf, calling out, "Skoodle, Skoodle!" but it was too late.

Dink *burbled* anxiously on Tom's shoulder.

Skoodle was gone.

Eva tapped me on the shoulder, "Everyone's watching."

"Here comes mum and dad."

I hardly noticed, even when the volleyball team came running.

"Charlotte," Tom whispered, "there he is," his voice trembled as he pointed to the washed up Goobie.

"Skoodle?" Fearing the worst, I reached out to shield the animal.

A crowd had formed a semi-circle around us.

"What is it?"

"It's a gerbil."

"No, it's not! It's a hamster."

"Move aside, move aside!" came a commanding voice. "Come on, give me some space."

"Mr Rogers!" Eva exclaimed. "Charlotte, Mr Rogers is our local vet. He's very good. We can trust him."

"Okay, everyone. Time to move off. Go on, off you go." Mr Rogers shooed at the small crowd, then crouched down to speak to me.

"Hello," he smiled kindly. "I'm Rick Rogers, the local vet. May I please look at your pet?"

"Skoodle's not a pet," I quietly told him. "Skoodle is free and wild and our friend." My eyes glistened.

"Let me see."

Mr Rogers looked up and hollered to someone coming up the beech, "Elena, drive my van onto the beach. We are taking…" he hesitated, "… Skoodle, is it?" he asked me. I nodded. "We are taking Skoodle to my surgery."

A tall blonde lady, dressed in casual clothes, nodded and ran to fetch the vehicle.

"Is everything alright?"

"Nothing we can't fix Mr Parsons."

Eva's parents greeted him warmly as he introduced himself to mum and dad.

"Can we come with you?" Eva asked Mr Rogers. "Oh, please, oh, please!"

Seeking approval from Josh and the others, he answered, "Of course, you must. I'll have you home for dinner."

The next thing I knew, we were in the van on our way to Mr Rogers' surgery.

Mr Rogers' Surgery

"Okay, let's plan this... Elena, can you open the practice?"

"With pleasure, Rick."

"Charlotte? Can you carry Skoodle through to the back? Just follow Elena."

"Okay."

"Eva, are you okay with the other Goobie?"

"Dink has settled down, so yes, without a doubt."

"Tom, I need you to help me once we are inside."

Tom looked worried, but he nodded.

Mr Rogers pulled into the car park and

we piled out of the van. The cool air chilled us.

As instructed, I followed Elena with Skoodle. Tom and Eva walked quietly behind us. We passed the pet section, went down a short, white-walled corridor and entered the surgery. It looked very clinical… cold… a little frightening, to be honest.

Mr Rogers entered from another room. "Tom, put these gloves on please."

Tom shook his head nervously, "I don't want to, Mr Rogers."

"I will," volunteered Eva, reaching for the gloves. "Here, Tom, you take Dink."

"Charlotte, can you put Skoodle on the bed?"

As I obeyed, Mr Rogers switched on an overhead lamp. It was so bright that for a moment – just a split second – Tom, Eva and I stepped back in surprise.

We couldn't believe what we saw. A blue plastic milk bottle ring was wrapped around Skoodle's body!

"Ocean pollution! I've had it with pollution."
Mr Rogers shook his head, "We have one
of the *cleanest* coastlines too."

"Is Skoodle breathing?"

"Faintly, Eva. Let's remove the plastic
and see if it will help."

Slowly, with a steady hand, the vet
carefully cut the blue plastic ring from
Skoodle's body.

A sudden unexpected jolt made Eva jerk her hand back in fear. We all watched intently, waiting for Mr Rogers to speak.

"Eva, could you gently massage this area? Like this…" he demonstrated, "start with the arms and work in small circles underneath, all the way to the chest."

Eva nodded and took over.

"Not too much pressure. Can you feel the heartbeat?"

"Hardly," she said, concentrating.

"Keep massaging. I'm going to make a quick call."

Mr Rogers stood leaning against the far counter as he made a call. It was so silent we could hear the dial tone.

"Hello, Mrs Hall speaking."

"Afternoon Mrs Hall, it's Rogers. I have a creature here… unusual…" there was a short, muffled pause then, "I'm sure you understand what I mean."

"Good gracious!" we heard her exclaim.
"How can I help?"

Mr Rogers turned his back to us so we couldn't overhear their conversation.

Eva sighed, "Gosh, I'm getting tired."

Dink burbled from within her hair.

"We're going to have to help, Tom. Gloves on," I told him.

"Yep, I'm in this time!" He confidently replied, slipping the gloves over his hands.

We took over from Eva, taking it in turns to gently massage the Goobie. It seemed like we were there for hours. I briefly wondered if mum and dad were worried, but was soon lost in my fears for Skoodle.

And so, the time passed.

8

Mrs Hall to the Rescue

The surgery was silent. Mr Rogers kept checking Skoodle's heartbeat and watching the clock.

Tom was slumped on the bench, his chin resting in his hands and his elbows on his knees. Dink perched on his head.

"Is Skoodle getting any better?"

"Hard to tell, Eva. Special help is on the way. Not too long to go."

"Whatever does he mean?" I whispered to Tom.

"How would I know? I'm never told anything first.

Beats me," he shrugged his shoulders.

"It feels like midnight but it's only 7 o'clock. I think I'll text Dan."

"Good idea, Charlotte. He needs to know."

"Yes, you're right, Tom."

SKOODLE ALMOST DROWNED.
@ THE VET. A PLASTIC RING
TRAPPED HIM IN THE WAVES.
WILL UPDATE SOON. C, T & E

The practice door opened.

Eva touched Tom's arm, "Sshhh… I can hear somebody talking."

We all sat up straight, straining to hear. Mr Rogers raised his head, stood up and crossed the floor to the door in big strides. We could hear shoes shuffling and lots of chatter. The door swung open and in marched Mr Rogers, Elena and, to my surprise, Mrs Hall!

"Mrs Hall," Mr Rogers began, "meet Eva, Tom and Charlotte."

"Hello, Eva," Mrs Hall greeted. She looked our way and raised an eyebrow, "Well I never… it's Charlotte and Tom!"

"Mrs Hall!" I burst out, louder than intended.

"Hello, my child," she said, "so the secret's out the bag, I see."

It certainly was…

What did this all mean? I wondered. She *wasn't even surprised to see Dink.*

Mrs Hall interrupted my thoughts.

"Right, where is Skoodle?"

I hesitated, unsure of what to say.

Mr Rogers passed Mrs Hall a lab coat.

"The Goobie is over here."

"How long has Skoodle been like this?"

"About three hours. His vitals have been stable but he has not moved. Not one bit."

"Right, children. Sit on the bench with – Dink, is it? – while we get to work."

We removed our gloves, walked to the bench and plonked ourselves down. Dink remained perched on top of Tom's head.

"I think I'll ring mum to let her know we're alright," Eva told us, moving off to the side.

"Can you ask what's for dinner?" Tom called after her as his stomach grumbled.

I decided to update Danny

> SKOODLE IS ALIVE BUT HASN'T MOVED. WE R TIRED & HUNGRY. POOR POOR SKOODLE. C, T & E

Dan replied almost instantly.

> CHARLOTTE! IS SKOODLE OKAY? KEEP ME POSTED? I'M WAITING UP. DAN

We sat and sat and sat until, finally, we heard…

Bur... Burr... Burrrble

"Skoodle!" we all shouted in delight, jumping up and rushing to his side.

Dink got there first.

9

Welcome Home

We arrived home before dark. Despite the chill in the air, the front door was wide open. Everyone was waiting inside… even Charlie.

"Here we go! Are you ready, Tom?" Mr Rogers asked as he parked the car.

"I'm ready."

"Girls? Ready?"

"Ready," we answered in unison.

We needed to get the Goobies upstairs as quickly as possible. They'd had quite an extraordinary day.

Elena opened the van doors and let us out the back. Mr Rogers took the lead, meandering slowly up the path. He turned periodically to check on us. Elena caught up to him as he stepped across the welcome mat...

...straight into a flood of questions...

"Where are the children?"

"Did the animal survive?"

"What was it?"

Mr Rogers took a deep breath and smiled. "May I introduce my cousin, Elena Lawton."

As she stepped forward to greet everyone, Tom bent his knees, twisted his waist sideways and darted between them to tag Charlie.

"Come on!" he said as he raced up the stairs, cradling his pockets. Only we knew that Skoodle and Dink were inside.

Eva and I distracted our parents so Tom could get away.

"Sorry! Excuse us," I mumbled, slipping past.

Eva was hot on my heels, "Coming through!"

"Girls, girls, what's the rush?" dad asked, raising his arms as he turned to avoid us.

Too tired for questions, we made our way to the kitchen as fast as we could.

"Let them go," mum said, "they're hungry."

"Would you like to come through to the lounge?" invited Paige.

"I'm sorry but we must get back. We wanted to make sure the children got home safely," Mr Rogers and Elena politely declined.

The rest of the conversation became muffled. We popped our heads around the corner to wave goodbye. They winked at us, waved back and disappeared out the door.

"The bowls have gone from the wardrobe, Eva," reported Tom and Charlie, joining us in the kitchen.

"That must be mum. Let me put them back, I'll be quick sticks."

"Well, I'm starving!"

"Me too, Charlotte!" Charlie said.

Paige, opening the fridge and selecting a few dishes, placed them on the counter.

"Let's eat!" Eva skipped into the kitchen, tapped her arm twice and joined in our feast.

"You don't have to tell me twice!" Tom smiled.

It tasted delicious! We were busy gorging ourselves when everyone else wondered in.

"Can Charlie stay over tonight?"

"Where will he sleep, Eva?" her dad replied.

"In my room! On the floor with Tom in sleeping bags. Pleeease?" she pleaded.

There was a pause…

"Well… as long as you leave the door open."

We couldn't believe our luck! We gathered a few midnight snacks and headed upstairs.

"What are we going to do about Skoodle and Dink if we leave the door open?" Tom whispered. "What about the cats?"

"Let's see what happens. Look at them now," I said, pointing at the two of them curled up together. They were fast asleep. "Sometimes you just have to let things solve themselves. They were hidden for so long at home, I'm sure they can take care of themselves here." I shrugged my shoulders and messaged Dan.

WE R HOME. SKOODLE IS FINE & RECOVERING. CHAT 2MORO. WE R EXHAUSTED. C, T & E

GOOD NEWS! THANX 4 THE UPDATE. CHAT 2MORO. DAN

It wasn't long before the night's chill and the day's events engulfed us, and we fell into a peaceful sleep.

10

A Restful Day at Home

"Wake up, wake up!"

"Get off meee!" I cried, opening my eyes.

"Sorry, Charlotte," Eva backed off a little, "but you need to wake up. Look, look! The Goobies have gone."

"What?" I sat up, leapt from the bed, grabbed my dressing gown and booted Tom and Charlie as I started frantically looking for Skoodle and Dink.

"Get up and help us!" Eva pleaded with them, pulling at their sleeping bags to make sure they were awake.

"Ahh!" yelped Tom, "What's happening?"

"The Goobies have gone! Help us search for them." Eva let go of the sleeping bags and headed out the bedroom door.

"Hurry!" my voice sharply echoed as I followed Eva.

The boys were up in a flash and, jumping the last step, we stood in the entrance hall listening.

Swoosh…

Whirl…

Meow!

… we followed the sound to the lounge…

… and burst into laughter!

Skoodle and Dink were playing Cat and Goobie chase around the sofa with Tippen and Naliyah.

"Morning," the babysitter greeted us in a chirpy voice, "those are lovely teddies! Where did you find them?"

We froze, looking left, then right, then left, then right again.

"Uuuuh…" I thought quickly, "from the Cotswolds," I said truthfully.

Tom and Eva carefully picked up Skoodle and Dink, who were both propped up in the corner of the sofa, looking just like teddy bears.

We nervously backed out of the room, hoping Mary would not ask for a closer look.

"OObies, OObies," Katie cooed behind us.

Phew! ... What a close call that was.

Eva had promised us a morning of arts and crafts, so we rushed upstairs to get dressed and headed straight for the conservatory.

We cleared the table, setting out all the tools and materials that we would need to make a sea-glass painting: a stencil, two pencils, paint, glue, coloured cardboard, canvas and – of course – all the sea glass that Eva had collected from the beach.

You will never believe what we made!

"Charlotte! Eva! Look what we did," Charlie beamed proudly. "Oh, those are nice," he said admiring our hearts.

"What have you done?" Eva casually asked.

"We thought we would make a poster on ocean pollution, especially plastics."

"Because of Skoodle," Tom piped up.

"It's quite serious you know," Charlie said earnestly. "Would you like to see it?"

When we nodded, Tom launched into an enthusiastic description of the poster with animated back-up from Charlie.

11

The Island Hunt

"Charlie's here! Can we go now?" Eva asked her dad, grabbing the small blue rucksack for Skoodle and Dink. She had enough energy for us all.

Josh threw his keys in the air, "Let's go!"

He teased Charlie with a few playful punches as he moved past him towards the front door.

"All aboard the stagecoach! Let the orangutan hunt begin."

Josh led the way. We couldn't help but laugh as Eva's contagious excitement spread.

"First stop, St Helier!" Tooting his horn twice, he shouted again, "All aboard."

I typed a quick message to Dan.

> GOING ON AN ORANGUTAN
> HUNT. SKOODLE & DINK 2.
> WILL UPDATE LATER! C, T & E

> HAVE FUN. DON'T GO NEAR
> THE SEA! DAN

I put my mobile in the rucksack and smiled as Skoodle and Dink seized the opportunity to float out and hide behind our hair.

We wriggled and giggled.

Competition time!

We'd hardly been driving for long when Tom, grinning from ear to ear, pointed shouting "I see one!"

"Pull over, dad, pull over!"

"Alright. We'll need to keep track of the number on it. Who's jumping out?"

"Tom's got a camera on his watch. Can't we all jump out? I'd love a closer look."

"Be quick, Charlotte."

"Take a picture, Tom, quick," I said, nudging him as Eva, Charlie and I brushed past to pose by the statue.

Next, we headed to Pier Road, beady eyes scanning the sidewalks. Eva's dad parked the car and we raced to the library.

"There's one, Tom!" Eva pointed.

"Here's another one," Charlie shouted.

"I'm coming, Charlie," Tom puffed, a little out of breath.

"And here's another one!" I added.

We marched to the square; walked through the market; explored the shops; had drinks in a café; visited the jewellers and toured the whole town. We had found ten orangutans!

"Onwards to St Aubins," Josh cried.

We laughed and sang all the way there, making up words as we went along.

"Listen, I've recorded us on my mobile."

The Orangutan Hunt

Rolling rumbles and rickety rocks
Orangutan hunt around the dOcks!
To the market, library and grocery store
We'll search the streets til our feet are sore!

Rolling rumbles and rickety rocks
Orangutan hunt around the dOcks!
Inland and towards the shore
We'll hunt and hunt til we can't anymore!

Rolling rumbles and rickety rocks
Orangutan hunt around the dOcks!
This fun competition is a friendly fight
To help the Orangutans with their plight!

We reached St. Aubins. Skoodle sank deep into the collar of my golf-shirt. Sea air and the rumbling of waves filled our senses.

"There, there, there," Eva pointed, "there's an orangutan over there."

There was an old man standing next to it taking a photo.

"Ooo competition," Josh teased.

"Come on!" I grabbed Eva's arm and raced up to it.

The old man was mounting his bike as we arrived. Dink floated over to the orangutan. He perched on top, watching the old man intently. I felt for Skoodle and relaxed - he was still on my shoulder.

"Watch out!" shouted Eva. "Catch Dink!"

"What?"

"Looooook!" she pointed wildly.

Before we'd had the time to blink, Dink had floated across and settled on the bicycle, which was already in motion. The old man happily peddling off, completely unaware.

Eva ran.

"Faster, Eva!" I hollered after her at the top of my voice.

Charlie was close behind Eva and Tom, with his head down, running full pelt; all of them trying desperately to reach Dink.

For a few moments, I thought Eva was gaining on him. But arms out, chest heaving, she finally admitted defeat and bent over, hands on knees, gulping in air.

Dink was gone!

12

Dink Makes the News

It was a gloomy afternoon. The dark heavy clouds blew in from across the ocean, and as we entered the house, we knew we had to act fast. A storm was coming.

We had to find Dink!

Charlie ran home for lunch, promising to return within the hour.

Tom trudged upstairs to fetch his hoodie. We heard him muttering apologies to our parents for losing his toy.

Eva and I made sandwiches in the kitchen before heading to the dining room – we were chatting about what to do next when Tom joined us.

"Have a sandwich, Tom," I passed him the plate, "we were just talking about our next move."

"Should we tell Mr Rogers?" Tom swallowed a mouthful of ham and cheese. "He knows about the Goobies."

I nodded, "I think he's our only hope."

Eva jumped up from the table, "Mum has his number. I'll get it."

Skoodle poked his head out from under my hair. He floated over to Tom, sliding into the cowl of his hoodie. Tom wriggled his shoulders to accommodate the Goobie.

Eva returned with Charlie; she was updating him on our plan.

"Good idea," Charlie said enthusiastically, "what do we tell them?"

"The truth of course! Where it happened; at what time. Let's write a description of the old man and his bike. That will help too."

"Good thinking, Eva. Tom, can you

message Dan and let him know what's happened?"

"Sure."

HI DAN. DINK'S MISSING!
TRYING 2 ORGANISE A SEARCH
PARTY. C, T & E

Eva called Mr Rogers while Charlie and I drew a quick map of the area where Dink disappeared.

"Mr Rogers is going to help. He said the Goobies are special and we need to protect them. He's picking up Elena and coming straight over."

"That's great, Eva. Charlie and I drew this map." I passed it around, "Can you think of anything to add?"

Tom shook his head, nudging Charlie, "We had better get on with the description."

CLUE

BLUE + YELLOW

HOUSES

RESTAURANTS

MAIN ROAD

LAST SEEN!

CLUE

SCOTCH CAP

BEIGE JACKET

JEANS

BLACK SHOES

STONE WALL

BICYCLE PATH

RUNNING

BIG TREE

ROCKS

BOATS

"A blue and yellow bike with large letters over the wheel," Eva spoke with conviction, "and it had a wicker basket on the back."

"The old man had a thin, beige jacket with a white shirt. He wore jeans."

Charlie wrote furiously.

"I'm sure I saw a cap or beret," reported Tom, "with black trainers."

"Can anyone remember the bike brand?"

"That's difficult, Charlie. I don't think I even looked," Tom said.

"I think we have enough," Charlie sighed placing the pen on top of the list.

"Now we wait for Mr Rogers." Charlotte put the information and map together ready for his arrival.

We sat on the floor playing a board game to occupy our minds. We could hear mum and Paige chatting over coffee in the kitchen. The television was on in the background.

'The International Flower Festival' the news headline echoed.

"Huh?!" Tom drew in a deep breath, "Look!"

Katie pointed, "OObie, OObie."

We turned to watch.

"What is it …?" My mouth fell open as I saw what he was looking at.

The doorbell rang.

Eva stood up, "I'll get it."

"Quick, Eva! Bring Mr Rogers. Hurry!" Charlie urged her, desperately gesturing for them to rush.

"Afternoon everyone!" greeted Mr Rogers, lifting his hand to wave as he was practically shoved in front of the tv.

"Look!" Tom pleaded again.

There, in front of us, on the news, amongst the crowd, was… DINK!

Oh no! Not 13.

I have been advised, by a reliable source, that a Chapter 13 would be ill-fated; especially if one were to read it on a Friday. We would not want to tempt fate in 2020. Personally, 13 is a lucky number!

14

Finding Dink.

We arrived in St Catherine's parish. The news crew were struggling to pack away their equipment. The sky had darkened and gusts of wind had driven the crowd back. People ran to their cars as slow, heavy raindrops fell from above. It was a warning. A big storm was about to hit.

"Can you see Dink?" Mr Rogers hollered over the howling wind.

"Dink?... Diiink..." Tom called in earnest.

Eva followed suit, cupping her hands around her mouth to make a funnel and crying out,

"Dink... Diiinnnk."

We leant into the wind, making our way to the spot where we last saw him on the news.

I looked around, hoping to catch a glimpse of feathers. It was chaotic! Umbrellas turning inside out, the camera crew bolting for their van, cars pulling out and **ZOOOOM**ing off... but no Dink.

Elena scaled a tree for a better vantage point, but the wind raged angrily around her and she couldn't see past the rain.

We called and called...

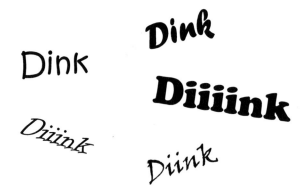

Eva battled with her raincoat as the rain pelted down; Tom's shoes *squelched* as we walked; even Mr Rogers looked *soggy*.

We almost gave up...

                ... then determination set in.

We decided to split up to cover more ground. Mr Rogers and Charlie teamed up to comb the area where the news was broadcast; Elena and Tom scoured the treeline. Eva and I headed toward the beach.

"What are we to do?"

Eva didn't reply - she couldn't hear me.

It was hard opposing the howling wind. We used hand signals to accompany our words, which were often whisked away.

"Come on, Eva! Let's check the beach."

"Dink won't be there," she raised her voice so I could hear, "It's raining, and the sea is choppy. I think he'll stay away."

"What do you suggest?"

"Follow me!" Eva ran into the wind and driving rain, hair streaming behind, her face reddening in the wet cold.

Heads down, we moved in the direction of a distant tower.

"Come on!" she hollered again, turning to give me a wave of encouragement. Eva's body twisted around, her left foot over balanced on a rock, and - for a split second - I held my breath hoping she wouldn't fall.

"Be careful!"

I was too late with a warning.

Her ankle twisted and gave way as she fell with a scream, hitting the ground hard.

"Oooowwww!" she howled.

"Eva!"

I ran to her side. Kneeling, I could see that she couldn't make it back on her own.

I placed Eva's left arm over my shoulder. Scanning the immediate area for shelter, I could only see a tree. *Well... it will just have to do!* I told myself, hauling Eva to her feet.

"We need to get to that tree," I mouthed to Eva, supporting her weight as we both hobbled inland.

We struggled, eventually reaching shelter. Huddling up against its trunk, we used my windbreaker as an umbrella to cover our heads. We were wet, cold and exhausted. Eva was grimacing in pain. Despite all this, we made our final attempt to call Dink.

We would have to sit the storm out... maybe 'til morning. I shuddered at the thought.

I didn't know if anyone would find us. Nestling close together, we pulled the windbreaker over our knees for warmth.

Wait! What was that? I lifted my head, straining to hear… faint voices - *Yes, that's it* - voices, carrying on the wind.

"Helloow? Charrrrrlotte…? Eeeevaaa…?"

"Did you hear that?"

"No." Eva's head stayed on her knees.

"Listen... through the crashing waves… I think I heard someone."

I could see she was distracted by the pain in her ankle.

"Stay here." I jumped to my feet, ran to the edge of the beach, and shouted into the wind, "Over heeere. We are here!" I waved my arms high and kept shouting, "We are here!"

I couldn't see a thing. It had gotten late and the storm-darkened sky swallowed the ocean.

I glimpsed a torch flashing through the haze of rain.

They had found us!

"Eva's hurt," I cried out.

"Where is she?"

I led them to the tree. We found Eva huddled up in a little pocket of warmth. Mr Rogers scooped her up and we made our way back.

"Did you find Dink?" I asked.

"Afraid not," Charlie sullenly replied.

I spotted Skoodle, who was tucked into Tom's hoodie, poking his head out in sorrow. No-one spoke… there was nothing to say. The chorus of the storm engulfed us.

"Something's wrong with Skoodle?"

"What do you mean?" puffed Mr Rogers, gently lowering Eva to the ground.

"He can't keep still," Tom began. "Watch out!"

Skoodle floated from Tom's shoulders to the ground before disappearing under the van.

"Skoodle," Tom called, kneeling on the floor. He looked underneath, then, much to our surprise, vanished too.

There was a **scuffle**, a **HOLLER**, a *splash* of mud, and, before Tom had any chance of wriggling out, Skoodle and Dink rose through the dampened air.

Dink had found us!

15

A Peaceful Day at the Zoo

"I'm back!"

We gasped seeing Eva's crutches.

She smiled, "It's not that bad; only a sprain."

Sitting in the lounge, pondering what to do for the day, our general thinking was to stay in.

"Pfff… not likely. A sprained ankle won't stop me from going out. We should go to the zoo!"

"Cool," Tom blurted out, "can Charlie come?"

Our parents agreed. "Please remind Charlie to bring his membership card."

After last night's storm, the day was fresh and sunny. I ran upstairs to see Skoodle and Dink. Sitting on the floor, I put on my shoes and began whispering their names... *"Skoodle... Dink..."*

Their response was instantaneous, jumping into my dress pockets before I left the room.

We entered the zoo at a steady pace, taking note of the variety of items on sale in the gift shop. It was abuzz with people. Worryingly, Skoodle and Dink would not keep still.

"Let's walk this way."

"Good idea, Tom. We can head towards the Reptile House."

"I'm scared of snakes Charlie," said Eva, hoping we would change direction.

"They can't hurt you. They're behind glass," laughed Charlie and Tom running to the amphibian house.

"Look, Eva, look!" I gushed excitedly, pointing at the meerkats.

We edged closer. Skoodle and Dink cautiously ventured from my pockets.

"They vanish so fast! Look how quickly they move," Eva said, hobbling along. "Do you think they'll be okay?"

We were like watchdogs, guarding them as they explored the meerkat desert.

Looking up, we saw Skoodle duck behind a rock and Dink dive into a burrow, a mob of meerkat pups in hot pursuit. It looked like the Goobies had the upper hand. We giggled at their antics as I quickly messaged Dan.

"Come on, Charlotte, let's walk on slowly. It'll give the others a chance to catch up."

"Skoodle! Dink!" I called, laughing as they tumbled towards us with the meerkat pups

"They keep us so busy! I am going to miss them when you return home," Eva sighed.

As we strolled past the restaurant and along the winding path, birdsong filled the air.

"That'll be the tropical birds," Eva said knowingly. "They're in big cages over there."

"Tag," Tom called, running past Charlie and jabbing him in the arm.

"Right back at you," bellowed Charlie, lunging forward to tag him back. He missed and the boys dashed off chasing each other.

Eva and I sauntered on with mum and Paige. We passed the gorillas but kept our distance – largely because of Skoodle and Dink – and soon came across orangutans swinging in their playground.

Entering the indoor enclosure, Eva and I stood together reading the information board aloud. It was all about orangutans losing their homes. It was heart breaking. Strangers stopped to listen. I felt shy but continued…

… just then, Tom and Charlie **burst** through the entrance. As the solemn atmosphere hit them, they stopped short and caught the tail end of what I was saying.

"Did you know all of that?"

"Well… not all of it," Eva admitted. "I knew about the habitat loss and deforestation."

As everyone shuffled out, I noticed some people leaving money in the donation jar and discretely added a pound of my own.

We left the orangutans and meandered down the path, passing all sorts of primates along the way – gibbons, howler monkeys, tamarins… my favourite were the lemurs! Tom and Charlie had us in fits of laughter as they bounced around with their fists raised in mock fight.

Next - a world of butterflies!

Entering the dome, we pushed past the plastic screens. Heat and humidity hit us.

"This is a different world! Are we still in Jersey?"

"Whooa," exclaimed Tom, "check out these flowers!"

"Look at the colour of the butterflies, too."

"Skoodle, Dink," Eva called as her arms

reached forward to stop them in the air.

The Goobies were enchanted by the butterflies and floated around them in wonder.

"Elena!" I called surprised to see her.

"Hello, everyone. Let me show you around the butterfly world."

It was magnificent! Elena explained all about the different butterflies and their lifecycles; the scales on their colourful wings and their long tongues that worked like straws. She even said they enjoyed mashed up bananas that had fermented a little.

Tom and Charlie screwed up their faces…

"Eeeew!"

"Gross!"

Butterflies kept landing on the daisies of Eva's jumper. Tom kept trying to photograph them. We loved every moment!

Waving goodbye to Elena, we drifted towards the museum.

"What's an aye-aye?" I asked, seeing it on the next sign.

Eva's eyes lit up. "Come on, I'll show you. They've got the biggest eyes!"

"Is that why they're called aye-ayes?"

"Noo," Eva grinned as we arrived at the door. The sign outside read

COMPLETE SILENCE.

We were eager to enter but our mums insisted on waiting outside for the boys, who were still quite captivated by the lemurs. We shrugged and went ahead.

I opened the door slowly and a beam of daylight cut through the darkness. We couldn't see anything... couldn't hear anything. Our senses were on high alert! The door swung shut. We stood near the entrance waiting for our eyes and ears to adjust. It was a bit spooky.

"Can you see the aye-ayes?"

Eva whispered.

"Over –" I began, but before I could say more, the door swung open and in came Tom and Charlie. Despite their attempts to remain quiet, the boys bubbled with energy. They forgot to wait for their senses to adjust and both stepped straight into the small confines of the room...

... and tripped over Eva's right crutch.

Clank... clank ....

"Aaaaa" came a cry.

"Sssshhhh" someone hissed.

Paige creaked open the door... Charlie was on the floor holding his leg. Tom was on all fours searching for the crutch. Eva leaned against the wall to prop herself up.

A movement caught my eye... I thought I'd caught a glimpse of Skoodle and Dink next to an aye-aye. My hands flew to my pockets.

Empty!

16

Recovery and Research

It was a day of rest.

Eva's ankle was worse after the incident with the aye-ayes and she had been told she HAD to rest. We decided to lie-low in her room with Skoodle and Dink instead. It wasn't too bad! We chatted endlessly about everything.

We were leaving tomorrow so I half-heartedly packed our rucksacks while we talked. Since leaving the zoo yesterday, we had spoken about little else.

"I thought the cocoons were awesome. Imagine going to sleep as a worm and waking up as a butterfly!"

"They're caterpillars, Tom," I corrected.

He poked his tongue out at me.

"When I first saw the butterflies, I was captivated too," said Eva. "I'm so glad Elena was there."

We all nodded enthusiastically.

"Did anyone actually see an aye-aye?" asked Tom inquisitively.

"I think I caught a glimpse of one."

"I definitely saw one. Its eyes were red."

"But you know where to look," I playfully teased Eva.

"Still lucky," said Tom.

"I think we missed out on the orangutan talk."

"Me too, Charlie."

"I felt so embarrassed reading out loud," I admitted. "I couldn't look at anyone."

"I was impressed, Charlotte. Everyone else was too," Eva replied cheerfully.

"So..." said Tom, "what did I miss?"

"Orangutans, habitat loss and palm oil!" I said, irritated.

"What's palm oil?" Tom scrunched up his face. "What do you mean?"

Eva and I began to explain, but Tom had so many questions! We all headed downstairs to research it.

We sat and read, and read and sat...

... there was just SO much to learn!

What palm oil is; how it is grown, harvested and used; the consequences of growing it unsustainably and how it affects where orangutans and other forest animals live.

We decided to make a poster so we could share this information with others.

"Orangutans need our help," stated Tom.

"Hmmm... maybe I could use this as my holiday assignment for school. Would any of you mind? I'll say it was a team effort."

"Sure, no problem, Charlotte." Eva grinned, "Let's make it a good one."

What an effort. It took us til the late afternoon to finish. Even Katie helped, in her own little way.

"I'm going to display it at the barbeque this afternoon," Eva said.

"Good idea," agreed Tom with enthusiasm.

Eva led the way, hobbling on her crutches, towards the pool area. We followed with the poster, Tippen and Naliyah padding behind us.

We found a good place to display it and stood back to admire our work. All of us but Tom, who was momentarily distracted.

"Wish we could swim," he sighed.

"Me too, Tom, but I think it's just too cold. Maybe next time," I said, crossing my fingers.

ORANGUTANS

HOME : RAIN FORESTS OF
        BORNEO AND SUMATRA

HABITAT : FORESTS

FOOD : FRUIT

CRITICALLY ENDANGERED!

WHY?

1. LOGGING

2. FIRES - DUE TO FARMING

3. PALM OIL
   → COOKING
   → COSMETICS
   → BIO-FUEL
   → FOOD PRODUCTS

HOW WE CAN HELP:

1. ADOPT AN ORANGUTAN

2. BUY SUSTAINABLE PRODUCTS

3. VOICE YOUR OPINIONS

4. SUPPORT ORANGUTAN PROJECTS

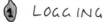

17

Farewells

We were up at the crack of dawn.

"Dad's getting stressed, Tom."

"I can hear." Tom pulled a funny face.

"We had better sort out Skoodle and Dink. We don't want them hurt or discovered or to escape again."

We ran upstairs to double check everything.

"Food," I called out.

"Check," said Tom.

"Small, comfortable blanket?"

"Check."

"Small bottle of water, sealed tight?"

"All ready."

Skoodle and Dink were gently placed inside the rucksack.

We followed Eva downstairs and sat on the grass outside watching Tom practice his gymnastics. We were all quite relaxed, despite knowing our departure was soon.

"Morning," called Charlie's mum and dad as they walked up the path with Charlie.

"Good morning," I greeted them, jumping up to help Eva to her feet.

"Hiya, Charlie," Tom grinned, finishing his last cartwheel.

Mum and dad joined us outside. Dad was laden with a suitcase in one hand and a rucksack in the other. Charlie's dad offered to help, but dad wouldn't hear of it. Instead, he huffed and puffed on his way to the car, mumbling all the while about being late.

"Have you packed everything, Charlotte? Tom?" he called back. "Claire, what about you? Everything packed?"

"Yes dear, all packed," mum said as she walked towards the car with Paige.

"Oh no! I forgot to say good-bye to Tippen and Naliyah," I said, racing inside to find them. Luckily, they were lying lazily by the front door. I gave them each a stroke and neither of them acknowledged me. I rolled my eyes and smiled.

"Okay, let's go!" I could hear dad say as he clapped his hands together.

I carefully shouldered my rucksack and joined the others in their goodbyes.

"Keep in touch and keep me updated."

"Sure will, Charlie." Tom said, closing the back door of the car and opening the window.

"Bye, Eva. Bye, Charlie." I gave Eva a big hug. "Thank you for everything." I tapped my arm in the sign of the Goobies and we all nodded and smiled. I waved a final goodbye as I climbed into the car, "Bye everyone."

"Right. We are off," Dad said, sighing in relief.

He put on the radio and turned it up – more 80's music. We loved it!

Peering out of the back window, we continued to wave. We were sorry to leave but happy to be going home. It was great to see Eva again, and now we had another friend too – Charlie.

As dad took a left turn toward St. Peters, we narrowly missed Mr Rogers and Elena coming up the lane. Dad had to stop.

"Gosh, I'm so glad we caught you," smiled

Mr Rogers, leaning out his window.

Elena leapt from the van excitedly and jogged up to the car. Tom and I jumped out to give her a hug goodbye.

"We'll miss you," we both said at the same time.

"Goodbye," Mr Rogers said sincerely, extending his hand to Tom.

"Goodbye, Mr Rogers. Thanks for all your help with Skoodle and Dink."

Turning to me, Mr Rogers winked and slipped an envelope into my hand as he shook it. I had no idea what was inside, but I took it quickly and concealed it in my pocket.

"Goodbye, Charlotte. Perhaps we'll see you in the Cotswolds," he smiled.

Chatting to our parents, Tom and I settled in the back.

"Gosh Tom, what a holiday!"

We arrived at the airport, dropped the rental car off and swiftly made our way through departures to the gate. Dad ushered us along the whole time, which saved the day as we boarded almost immediately.

I hoped Skoodle and Dink were okay – we hadn't had a chance to check on them since we left. A sudden thought struck me… *What if they escaped and we've left them behind?*

My hand flew to the bottom of my rucksack… I held it there, cradling the base and waited... and waited... and waited. Nothing! Cold dread filled the pit of my stomach. No, wait! There! Yes - a little jiggle… not much, but enough to know they're inside. I sighed the biggest sigh of relief. Even strangers looked my way, but I did not mind one bit.

Before we knew it, we were taking off. I pouted as the lady seated in front of me reclined her seat. It gave me less room.

"Grrr," I moaned to Tom.

He ignored me. "How is Skoodle and Dink?"

"They're fine. We can check on them a little later."

"Why not now?"

"NO!" I retorted, trying to open the little table so I could put my drink down.

When Tom didn't respond, I glanced his way. He had a look of horror on his face.

I turned my head slowly, following his gaze, and froze.

"Dink is out of the rucksack."

The Goobie was perched on top of the seat in front of me.

"How on Earth did Dink get there? I'm sure I shut my bag. Catch Dink!" I whispered urgently. I couldn't believe this was happening again!

Tom made a silent grab for Dink, but the Goobie disappeared. As he missed, I leapt up from my seat, accidentally knocking my table and sending my drink flying through the air. It sailed forward and landed with a very unfortunate **SPLAT** on the lap of the lady in front of me.

"*Aahhh,*" she screeched, throwing her arms in the air.

"Sorry, sorry, so sorry," I hastily apologised, fumbling for a napkin.

"Wretched children," she cursed.

I discretely glanced over her seat to look for the Goobie, but Dink was nowhere to be seen. I did see the lady though…

We laughed as she stormed off down the aisle looking for the toilet.

"I'm so glad I ordered water," I said to Tom, looking up... mum was glaring at me. "I'm in trouble." I slowly shrank into my seat hoping **the look** was all the punishment I would get.

Tom quietly sunk in his seat and whispered, "What about Dink?"

"We can't do anything with everyone watching." I bit my bottom lip.

"Okay." Tom pointed, looking confused. "Isn't that Dink?"

Sure enough, when I glanced down at my rucksack, two sets of big marble eyes were watching us from the dark.

I blinked.

"Wait... what just happened?"

Tom shrugged and put his headphones on.

What a flight!

18

Home Re-unions

"Open the gate, Tom."

These were the first words spoken on our journey home. Mum and dad were still cross from the commotion on the aeroplane.

Tom shrugged and got out the car. "EedwAAARD," he boomed.

Edward came bounding down the driveway with so much excitement that he could not stop wriggling.

Opening the door, I took a deep breath of the fresh air. We were home.

Edward bounced around the car, colliding into me as we met. I fell to the ground laughing.

Dad drove up to the front door.

"Tom, let's go to the stables to see Crackers."

I spun around to keep up with him, skipping and running towards the yard.

"We are out of sight, Tom. Let's let Skoodle and Dink out."

I opened the rucksack and, as they leapt out, a sudden Goobie crowd appeared! Goobies came from the greenhouse, the stables and even the fields – with no bother from Edward at all.

It was a Goobie reunion.

"Wow, Tom! Look at that."

We stood transfixed, rooted to the spot.

"I've missed home. It's so good to be back."

Crackers, cantering around the field, kept approaching the fence. I could see he was excited to see us and ran to him. Edward was hot on my heels.

Tom waited, watching the Goobies until the last one disappeared into the countryside.

"I'm getting cubes for Crackers," he hollered from across the yard. He jumped as he ran and, in no time at all, was ducking between the fence to join us.

"I hope the Goobies visit soon, Charlotte. I shall miss Skoodle and Dink."

"Me too." I put the halter on Crackers, "Come on, let's all go check on the chickens."

19

An Unexpected Call

We were all in the lounge…

… I was on the floor, sitting with one leg under my bottom and the other stretched out in front of me.

… Edward had rolled onto his back with his legs in the air - we were playing. I tapped his mouth and he tried to catch my hand.

… Tom had his head on the sofa arm and his body sprawled out. He was playing on his console - a superhero game, I bet.

… Dad had fallen asleep, plank style, with his head carefully balancing on the back of the sofa. His body looked extra-long, lengthening towards his feet where one ankle crossed the other on the floor.

His bright red socks caught my eye - I was so glad he was wearing them as they were a Christmas gift from me. I smiled.

… Mum sat in the single armchair, legs tucked up under her, reading a novel.

It was calm and peaceful.

I sighed… *I wonder what Skoodle and Dink are up to. Will they come visit? Will we see them again?*

Lost in my thoughts with my back against the sofa, sinking into the soft carpet, I felt myself falling asleep. Holidays are great, but nothing compares to home comforts.

DDDRRRRRINGG!!!

The landline rang, startling me awake. Edward and I sat up abruptly.

"Answer the phone, someone," I mumbled. I looked around sleepily and heard dad grunt.

"I'm not moving."

"Tooom," I pleaded, but he was so engrossed in his game that he didn't hear me. I turned to look at mum. Her book had fallen to her chest, her head tilted backwards. She was obviously fast asleep.

"MUUUM!" I called louder.

"Okay, okay," she yawned, "I'll answer it."

I felt a bit guilty until my curiosity kicked in. I could only hear mumbled conversation in the hall, but it was followed by laughter. After a few minutes, mum walked into the lounge wearing the biggest grin.

I raised an eyebrow, "Who was that?"

"That was Rachel," mum beamed before continuing, "it's been confirmed."

"What has?" Dad opened his right eye, "What's confirmed?"

The change in his tone caught Tom's attention. He looked up from his game, expectantly.

"Well… that was Rachel Butterworth."

"Yyyeeess," dad lifted his chin.

I interrupted, "That's Dan's mum, isn't it?"

"Shush," dad replied, glaring at me.

"Welllll…" mum said again, drawing it out… she raised both arms in the air in excitement and squealed…

My jaw dropped as a wave of excitement
hit me. I looked at Tom – he was sitting on

the edge of the sofa with his mouth open; his game forgotten on the side.

Dad sat upright.

Edward obviously picked up on our energy as he bounced between us.

Mum had our full attention.

"Who's going to Africa?"

we chorused together…

… from the corner of my eye I could see three Goobies peering through the lounge window. It wasn't Skoodle or Dink, but I was too distracted to pay attention.

We wanted to know…

… who is going to Africa?!

Prelude to

The GOObieS go Wily Africa

Charlotte jumped back. "What's that?" she asked, pointing a shaking finger. "Is it a snake?"

A sudden silence descended on the camp. Then it exploded with whistles and hollers as everyone tried to cram into the same space to catch a glimpse of the reptile.

"What's happening?" called Tom from the tent.

"Quick, Tom, quick! There's a snake!"

An almighty rustling could be heard from inside the tent as Tom fumbled his way out, clutching a camera.

Join Charlotte, Thomas, and the GOObieS on an African adventure in the wild, discovering new friends and the strangest animals!

Meet Jaimie, I'yaan, Thandei, Thaka and the new GOObie clan.

GOObie Adventures series

Out of the Woodland,
Cotswolds

Beyond the Woodland,
Jersey Channel Islands

The GOObieS go Wild
Africa

Book four takes the GOObieS on a walkabout in Australia.

Visit our web site and drop us a line, we would love to hear from you!

www.goobieadventures.com

Printed in Great Britain
by Amazon